A Where-in-the-Bible adventure book

Where is Jesus?

RHONA PIPE

Illustrated by Chris Masters

HARVEST HOUSE PUBLISHERS
Eugene, Oregon 97402

When Jesus is a few weeks old
Wise men come and give him gold.

? *Can you find three bags of gold?*
And can you see two other gifts—
a box of precious cream, called myrrh,
and a jar of sweet-smelling frankincense?

This story is in Matthew chapter 2 verses 1-12.

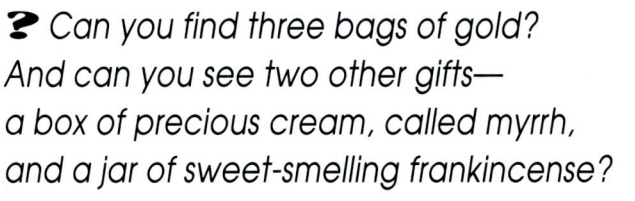

Jesus' mother is full of fear.
She's lost Jesus. He's not here.

Three days hunting all around
Till she finds him safe and sound.

❧ *Twelve-year-old Jesus is in the Temple,
talking to the teachers. Can you find him—
and his mother?*

This story is in Luke chapter 2 verses 41-50.

Oh, my! What a catastrophe!
The guests drank all the wine, you see.

But thanks to Jesus, all is fine.
He turns water into wine.

? *It was a disgrace to run out of wine at a wedding party.*
Find six tall water pots for the servants to fill with water.

This story is in John chapter 2 verses 1-11.

Very early in the day,
Jesus goes outside to pray.
His friends start hunting here and there.
Can you find him anywhere?

❓ *Can you also find four lambs that are lost?*

This story is in Mark chapter 1 verses 35-37.

All those hungry people there,
Sitting in the open air.

"Here's their supper," Jesus said.
"Two small fish, five loaves of bread."

❓ *Find two fish and five small loaves. Jesus fed
over five thousand people with this food.
Find twelve baskets for all the leftovers.*

This story is in Mark chapter 6 verses 30-43.

When the children come one day,
Jesus' friends all quickly say,
"Run along. Run along now, do.
Jesus has no time for you!"

But Jesus says, "You've got it wrong,
Let the children come along."

? *Can you find ten children who have left and must come back? They are crying.*

This story is in Mark chapter 10 verses 13-16.

Blind Bartimaeus cannot see.
He calls out loudly, "Please help me!"
"Be quiet, you!" the people sneer.
"You're not why the Lord is here."

But Jesus says, "Bring him to me.
I will make the blind to see."

❓ Can you find Bartimaeus' begging bowl,
his dirty old cloak, and his stick?
He doesn't need them now.

This story is in Luke chapter 18 verses 35-43.

Where's Zaccheus? Can you see?
He's climbed into a sycamore tree!
All the people laugh no end—
But Jesus says, "I'll be your friend."

❓ *Find Zaccheus up a tree, and his money bags—*
one, two and three. Can you see Jesus in the crowd?

This story is in Luke chapter 19 verses 1-10.

Jesus rides through all the crowd.
And the people sing aloud,
"Jesus is our king today,
Let's shout for joy along the way."

? *Jesus' enemies are angry when he rides into town on a donkey.*
Can you find eleven very angry men?

This story is in Luke chapter 19 verses 28-40.